PUFFIN BOOKS
Published by the Penguin Group: London, New York, Australia,
Canada, India, Ireland, New Zealand and South Africa
Penguin Books Ltd, Registered Offices: 80 Strand, London WC2R 0RL, England

puffinbooks.com

First published by Abelard-Schuman Ltd 1982
Published in Puffin Books 1984
Revised edition with new artwork published in hardback
by Macmillan Children's Books 2007
Revised edition published in paperback in Puffin Books 2008
This edition published in Puffin Books 2014

001

ISBN: 978–0–723–29935–6

Dear Zoo

Rod Campbell

PUFFIN

I wrote to the zoo
to send me a pet.
They sent me an ...

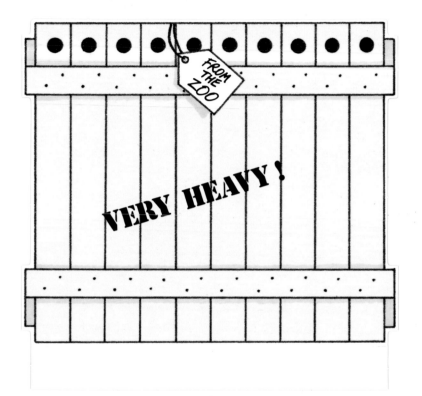

He was too big!
I sent him back.

So they sent me a …

He was too tall!
I sent him back.

So they sent me a ...

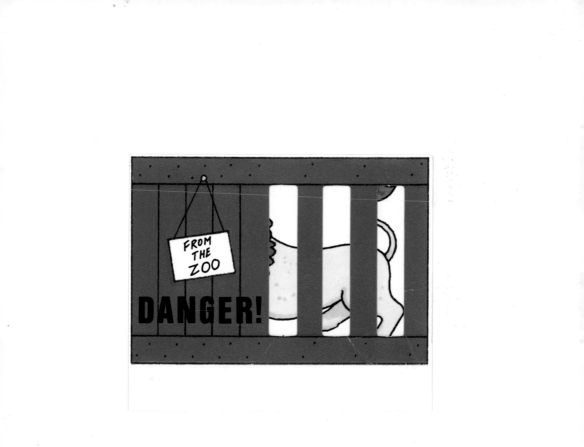

He was too fierce!
I sent him back.

So they sent me a ...

He was too grumpy!
I sent him back.

So they sent me a ...

He was too scary!
I sent him back.

So they sent me a ...

He was too naughty!
I sent him back.

So they sent me a …

He was too jumpy!
I sent him back.

So they thought
very hard, and
sent me a ...

He was perfect!
I kept him.